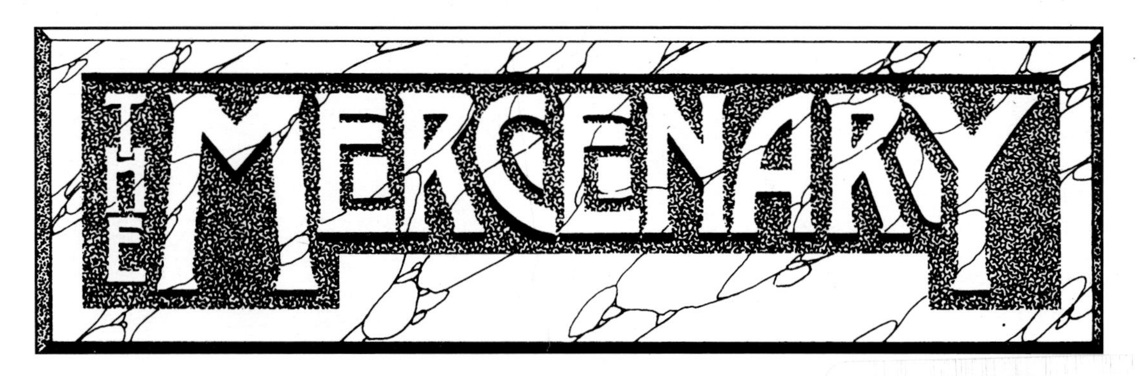

LOST CIVILIZATION
V. SEGRELLES

NANTIER • BEALL • MINOUSTCHINE
Publishing inc.
new york

Also available in the
Mercenary series:
The Cult of the Sacred Fire / The Formula: $14.95
The Trials / The Sacrifice: $14.95
The Fortress: $9.95
The Black Globe: $9.95
The Voyage: $10.95
Year 1000: $11.95
(Add $3 P&H 1st item, $1 each addt'l)

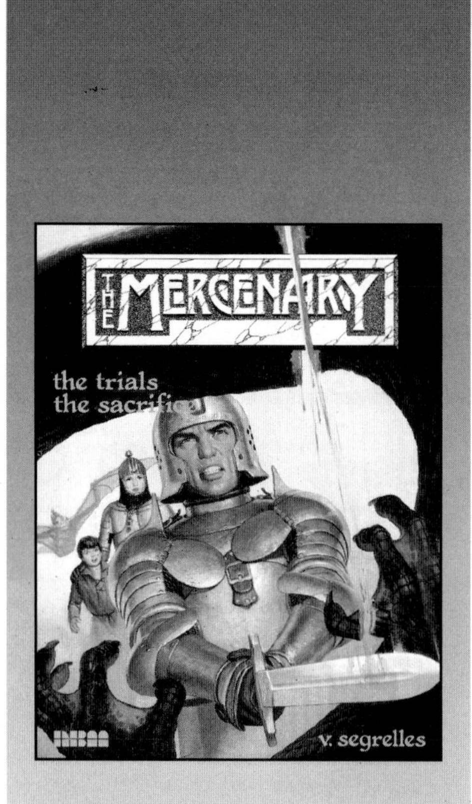

We have over 150 graphic novels in
print, write for our color catalog:
NBM
185 Madison Ave. Suite 1504
New York, NY 10016
http://www.nbmpub.com

ISBN 1-56163-198-1

Translation by Robert Legault
Lettering by CompuDesign
Printed in Holland

NANTIER • BEALL • MINOUSTCHINE
Publishing inc.
new york

THE YEAR 1003, WHEN SPAIN WAS DIVIDED IN TWO PARTS: TO THE SOUTH, THE ARABS, WHO HAD INVADED THE PENINSULA, AND TO THE NORTH THE CHRISTIANS, WHO WERE RECONQUERING IT. IN CHRISTIAN TERRITORY, NOT FAR FROM THE BORDER, IT'S DAWN...

THE TESTS HAVE PROVED THAT THIS GIRL IS A WITCH. WE SHALL BURN HER SO THE DEMON WON'T SPREAD AMONG US. MAY SATAN CLAIM HER SOUL!

IT'S NOT RIGHT. THIS IS A FARCE.

SILENCE, SINNER! YOUR PARENTS HAVE ALREADY BEEN BURNED AS HERETICS. NOW YOU WILL SUFFER THE SAME FATE.

YOU KNOW ME. TELL THEM I'M INNOCENT.
YOU MUST KNOW WHAT YOU'VE DONE...

HALT! STOP THIS!
HUH? WHO DARES TO INTERRUPT THE DIVINE RITES?

I, BEELZEBUB! PRINCIPE DEI. AVERNO!
FFFFSS!

YOU HAVE CALLED ME. BUT I SHALL NOT LIMIT MYSELF TO CARRYING OFF THE SOUL OF THIS YOUNG WOMAN...

YOU HAVE BEEN A GOOD SERVANT OF MINE, IT IS UNFORTU- NATE, BUT YOUR TIME IS FINISHED...I HAVE COME TO SEEK YOUR SOUL: IT BELONGS TO ME.

IT'S NOT TRUE! YOU LIE! I AM A SERVANT OF THE LORD!

A SERVANT OF THE LORD? IF ALL THE CLERGY WERE LIKE YOU, I WOULD ALREADY BE RULER OF THIS WORLD.

I AM YOUR LORD! AND I DECIDE WHAT TO DO WITH YOU, BELLACO.

IT IS TIME TO CARRY OUT THE SENTENCE.
AURG!!

GRRR...

GOD PROTECT US.
HAVE MERCY! I WAS ONLY CARRYING OUT THE COUNT'S ORDERS.

AURG!
YES, ANOTHER OF MY FAITHFUL SERVANTS. ORDER TO THE PYRE ALL WHO BAR HIS WAY!

MERCY! HAVE MERCY!
GRRR...

HALT, SATAN! ONLY GOD MAY JUDGE!
YOU AGAIN!

I HAVE COME TO STOP AN INJUSTICE. YOU KNOW VERY WELL THAT THE YOUNG GIRL IS INNOCENT.
DAMNED MEDDLER! WHAT DOES IT MATTER? THERE'S ALWAYS ROOM FOR ONE MORE SOUL IN HELL! DRAGON, LET GO OF THAT IDIOT AND FINISH OFF GEORGE.

YOU ALREADY KNOW THAT YOU'VE NEVER BEEN ABLE TO FINISH ME OFF.
WE'LL SEE ABOUT THAT!

DIE, MONSTER!

AURG!
NO!

CURSE YOU! YOU HAVE KILLED MY DRAGON.

IT DOESN'T MATTER...
FSSSSS...

HATRED AND EVIL WILL CAUSE MY DRAGON TO BE REBORN. WE'LL BE BACK.
FFFSSSSS...

THIS WOMAN IS INNOCENT. UNTIE HER.

TELL THE COUNT TO BE CAREFUL. WHEN HE LEAST EXPECTS IT, DIVINE JUSTICE WILL STRIKE HIM DOWN.

AND IF YOU EVER UNJUSTLY ACUSE ANY GIRL OR HER FAMILY, THE WRATH OF GOD WILL BE UPON YOU!

YOU MAY GO. AND DO NOT RETURN TO THIS ACCURSED PLACE.

WE SHALL DO AS YOU SAY, SIR.

MISTRESS, HOW FRIGHT-ENED I'VE BEEN.
STEP OVER HERE A MINUTE...I MUST SPEAK WITH YOU.

WE ARE STILL IN DANGER, CHILD. WE MUST FLEE AS SOON AS POSSIBLE. THANKS TO YOUR GRANDFATHER, YOU'RE ALIVE, BUT WHAT HAPPENED TODAY WILL SOON BE ONLY A LEGEND, AND THE COUNT WILL RETURN TO HIS OLD WAYS.

*IN THAT ERA THE MOSLEM EMPIRE WAS THE MOST ADVANCED IN THE CIVILIZED WORLD.

*TARTESANS: MYSTERIOUS ANCIENT CIVILIZATION THAT FLOURISHED IN THE SOUTHERN IBERIAN PENINSULA AND DISAPPEARED AROUND 500 B.C.

I COPIED IT AS EXACTLY AS I COULD...I KNOW IT'S NOT PAYMENT ENOUGH FOR WHAT YOU'VE DONE FOR ME...
YOU OWE US NOTHING, RAMIRO.

AND IN MY CASE I ASSURE YOU THIS IS AN EXCEPTIONAL PAYMENT.

YOU UNDERSTAND THAT LANGUAGE?
OF COURSE. HERE IT SAYS, "THE EARTH WAS FLOODED WITHOUT CEASING. LIFE WAS IMPOSSIBLE ON THE ISLAND. WE DECIDED TO ESTABLISH OURSELVES HERE BUT THE TARTESANS FOUGHT US OFF. WE SHALL GO FARTHER EAST."

LOOK! IT CONTAINS THE EXACT LOCATION OF ATLANTIS IN THE MIDDLE OF THE OCEAN, AND WHAT'S MORE, IN THE UNITS OF MEASUREMENT USED ON MY PLANET, THERE'S NO DOUBT THAT THIS TEXT IS AUTHENTIC.

I KNEW IT! THEY'RE FROM ANOTHER WORLD!

FROM YOUR PLANET...IT'S ROUND, RIGHT?...THAT MEANS THE EARTH IS ROUND, THEN?
YES, ALL THE PLANETS ARE SPHERICAL.

AND THEY SPIN AROUND THE SUN, RIGHT?
THAT'S CORRECT, RAMIRO. BUT HOW DO YOU KNOW THAT? YOU'RE AHEAD OF YOUR TIME.

ARISTARCHUS OF SAMOS, SECOND CENTURY B.C. ALL YOU HAVE TO DO IS READ IT. THE REST IS EASY.
NOW I KNOW WHY YOU'RE SO DANGEROUS: YOU KNOW TOO MUCH. YOU DO WELL TO LEAVE.

WE TOO ARE GOING. IF WE WANT TO TRAVEL UNOBSERVED, IT'S BETTER TO GO BY NIGHT.

THIS CAN'T BE ATLANTIS. PLATO SPOKE OF A GREAT CONTINENT, AND THIS IS ONLY A VOLCANIC ISLAND.
PERHAPS SO. ACCORDING TO THE TEXT THERE WAS FLOODING...LOOK, THAT LOOKS LIKE A CITY.

I STILL DOUBT IT'S WHAT WE'RE LOOKING FOR. THE ATLANTEANS MUST BE MORE ADVANCED...THOSE ARE BARELY HUTS.

NO, LOOK, THEY'RE ALL THE SAME. THEY'RE MADE IN A PATTERN: A LOGICAL SOLUTION TO AN URGENT PROBLEM.

THE LAND WAS FLOODING AND IT WAS NECESSARY TO RELOCATE TO THE HIGHER AREAS. THE REAL ATLANTIS IS UNDER THE SEA.

A SOLID MATERIAL, LIGHT, AND BY THE LOOKS OF IT RESISTANT TO THE HEAT OF LAVA. THIS CAN ONLY BE THE WORK OF YOUR ANCESTORS.

I FEAR THAT NO ONE IS LEFT IN THIS CITY.

NOT A SINGLE BODY, NOT A BOOK, NOTHING. THE CITY WAS EVACUATED IN AN ORDERLY MANNER, BUT WITH-OUT LEAVING ANY CLUES TO THEIR DESTINATION.
WE STILL HAVEN'T LOOKED UP THERE IN THAT MONOLITH.

WHAT'S THAT, A MONUMENT TO A SHARK?
I DON'T KNOW. IN ANY CASE, IT MAY BE A MARKER.

MERCENARY, COME HERE. LOOK WHAT'S IN HERE!

DAMN!
I THINK THERE'S NO NEED TO LOOK FURTHER.

JUDGING BY THIS GUY, THEY MUST HAVE LEFT A LONG TIME AGO.

LOOK! HE WROTE SOMETHING JUST BEFORE DYING. CAN'T BE A DIDLEY. MAYBE HE'LL GIVE US THE ANSWER.

"TO ALL OUR EXPLORERS. I, LAST GUARDIAN OF THE CITY, AND AT THE BRINK OF DEATH, WISH TO GIVE NOTICE THAT THE EVACU-ATION HAS TAKEN PLACE AHEAD OF THE SCHEDULED DATE."

"THERE WAS AN ERUPTION SO STRONG THAT IT HAS CONVINCED SOME OF US THAT THE LAST EXPLOSION IS IMMINENT. IT HAS ALSO DESTROYED THE GIANT SHIP WE HAD SO MUCH HOPE IN. THE GRAND COUNCIL IS SPLIT, AND THEY HAVE DECIDED TO EVACUTE IN TWO DIRECTIONS."

THIS INDICATES TWO OPTIONS, BUT NEITHER GUARANTEES THE ATLANTEANS ARE STILL AROUND...
I PROPOSE WE SPLIT UP AND EXPLORE EACH ONE.

ALL RIGHT. LET'S LOOK FOR FODDER FOR THE MOUNTS...WHAT'S THAT?

THESE TRACKS ARE RECENT. SOMEONE HAS BEEN HERE BEFORE US.

THOSE TRACKS...THAT'S PRETTY DAMN SPOOKY.
FORGET IT! WE HAVE TO REST FOR THE LONG VOYAGE.

MERCENARY, I WILL GO EAST.
ANY SPECAL REASON?
YES, IT'S FARTHER AND ACROSS THE DESERT. I HAVE MORE EXPERIENCE AT LONG-DISTANCE NAVIGATION.

ALL RIGHT. BUT JUST TAKE A LOOK AROUND AND COME BACK. WE'LL MEET HERE IN SIX DAYS. IF EITHER OF US IS DELAYED MORE THAN TEN DAYS, THE OTHER WILL GO LOOKING FOR HIM OR HER.

OK. BUT NO HEROICS. IF YOU'RE IN TROUBLE, SET DOWN IN THE SEA. THESE ANIMALS FLOAT VERY WELL. AND, MOST IMPORTANTLY, FOLLOW NORMAL SECURITY PROCEDURES SO WE WON'T MISS HOOKING UP.
YOU SHOULD KNOW ME BY NOW...

BE CAREFUL.

THE ISLAND TO THE SOUTH-SOUTHEAST, AS IT APPEARED ON THE MAP.

AHOY! LAND AT LAST.

A FLAT COASTLINE, WITH NO REFERENCE POINTS. LET'S FIND MY LOCATION.

PERFECT. NOW A STRAIGHT LINE WEST...

THIS IS FRIGHTENING. I LEAVE ONE SEA AND ENTER ANOTHER.

DAMMIT, THE DAY IS DONE, AND I HAVEN'T FOUND THEM....WAIT. WHAT'S THAT?

IT MUST BE THEM.

FOR THE MOMENT I CAN'T SEE. I'LL FLY LOWER UNTIL I SEE A CLEARING TO LAND IN AS CLOSE AS POSSIBLE TO THE CITY.

THERE ARE NO CLEARINGS IN THIS JUNGLE. I DON'T KNOW HOW I CAN...

MY GOD! WHAT A SETUP!

I CAN'T GET THROUGH THE JUNGLE WITH THE DRAGON. I'LL HIDE HERE A MOMENT.

BETTER TAKE A LOOK AROUND.

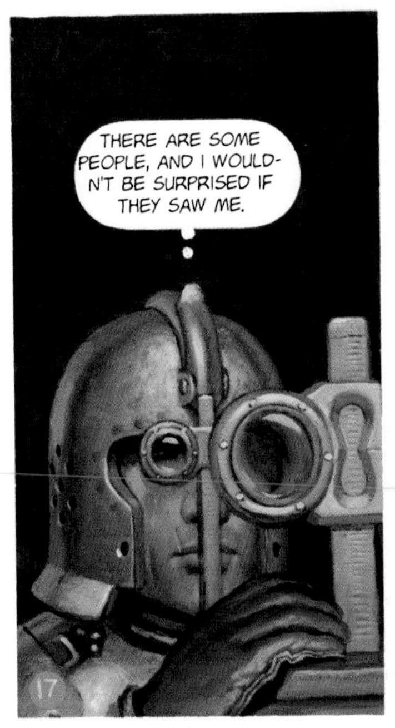
THERE ARE SOME PEOPLE, AND I WOULDN'T BE SURPRISED IF THEY SAW ME.

WHETHER THEY'VE SEEN ME OR NOT, THERE'S NO SENSE IN LOOKING FOR ANOTHER CLEARING...

*KUKULKAN: A MAYAN DIVINITY WHOSE NAME MEANS "PLUMED SERPENT." HE WAS CALLED QUETZALCOATL BY THE AZTECS.

I HOPE THIS IS CONVINCING.

HERE COMES MY AUDIENCE.

PARDON ME, SIR, BUT I MUST ASK WHO YOU ARE AND WHETHER YOU HAVE ANYTHING TO DO WITH THE ATLANTEANS.

THE ATLANTEANS? HEAVEN HAS CONFUSED YOU. I HAVE BEEN SENT BY KUKULKAN. I COME TO WITNESS THE SACRIFICE TOMORROW.
GRR..

FORGIVE ME, SIR, PLEASE FORGIVE ME, I HAD TO ASK.

PLEASE, SIR, WAIT WITH US, WE ARE BRINGING A THRONE.

BY GOD, THIS IS A FINE MESS I'VE GOTTEN INTO.

YOUR MAJESTY, KUKULKAN'S ENVOY HAD BEEN PLACED IN THE SOUTH PALACE AND IS UNDER GUARD, AS YOU ORDERED.

AND THE FLYING SERPENT?
IN THE PALACE GARDENS-- IT IS NOT A SERPENT. IT IS AN UNFAMILIAR CREATURE, BUT IT IS DOCILE AND OBEDIENT.

AND WHAT IF THIS MAN IS AN ATLANTEAN TRYING TO FOOL US?
AN ATLANTEAN DRESSED IN SILVER, MOUNTED ON AN ANIMAL THAT MAY BE BE COMPLETELY DIVINE? I DON'T THINK SO, YOUR MAJESTY.
YOU HAD BETTER BE RIGHT, UXMAL. YOU KNOW VERY WELL THAT YOUR POSITION IS HANGING BY A THREAD. YOU MAY GO.

IZAMAL. WHAT DO YOU MAKE OF THIS?
I DON'T KNOW...HE CAME FROM THE EAST, AND YOU KNOW WHAT THE SCRIP-TURES SAY. HE COULD ALSO BE AN ATLANTEAN GOD COME FOR REVENGE.

WHATEVER HE IS, WE CAN'T TAKE ANY CHANCES. TOMORROW DURING THE CEREMONY I WANT OUR THRONES SEPARATED AND GUARDS ALL AROUND ME.

I CAN'T STAND THE KING ANY MORE. ONE OF US HAS GOT TO GO...

TAM TAM TAM

THE SUMMONS TO THE PEOPLE...I HOPE KUKULKAN WILL APPROVE OF THE CEREMONY.
I HOPE SO TOO. KUKULKAN HAS SENT ME TO OBSERVE WHETHER THE TRADITIONS ARE BEING FOLLOWED.

EVER SINCE THE TOLTEC PEOPLE CAME TO THIS LAND AND CONQUERED THE MAYAS, WE HAVE OFFERED THE GODS HUMAN BLOOD.
I KNOW, I KNOW.

WE'RE IN AN UNCOMFORTABLE PERIOD OF PEACE, AND WE DON'T HAVE ANY PRISONERS OF WAR TO SACRIFICE...BUT WE'LL FIX THAT SOON...
MEANWHILE, WE'RE GOING TO SACRIFICE THIS LITTLE GIRL-FRIEND OF THE ATLANTEANS. WE'VE ELIMINATED ALL OF THOSE WRETCHES...NO, NOT TRUE, ONE ESCAPED.

DAMN! IT'S THE SAME SITUATION AS A FEW DAYS AGO, WITH THE JEWISH GIRL, AND I'M POWER-LESS TO SNATCH HER OUT OF IT.

THOSE GUARDS HAVE THEIR EYES ON ME. I CAN TELL THEY DON'T TRUST ME. ALL I'VE GOT IS A KNIFE. TRYING ANYTHING WOULD BE SUICIDE.

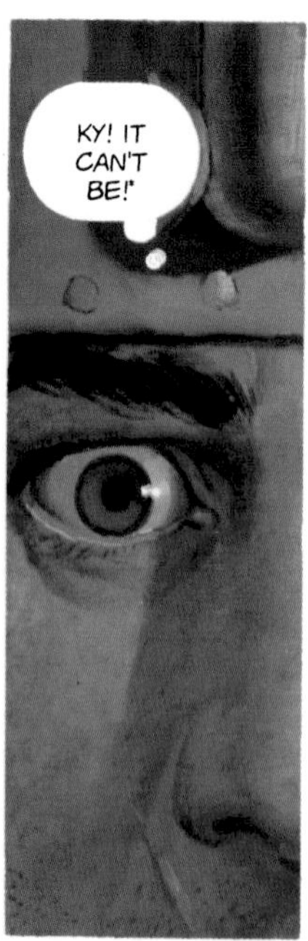

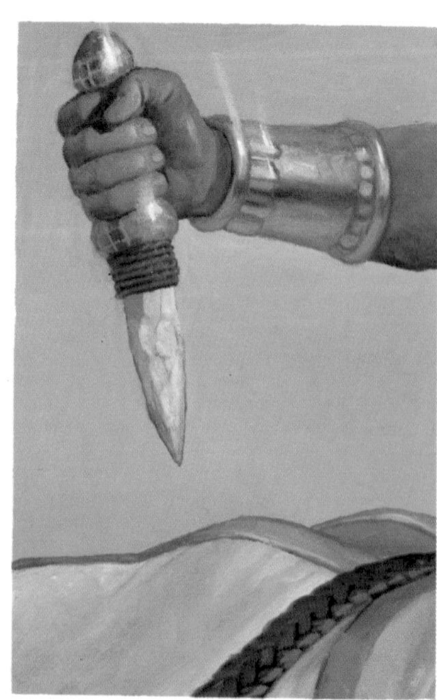

'THE VESSEL THAT THE PRIEST HOLDS UP IS IN REALITY THE WEAPON BELONGING TO KY, A CHARACTER WHO APPEARS IN "YEAR ONE THOUSAND, THE END OF THE WORLD."

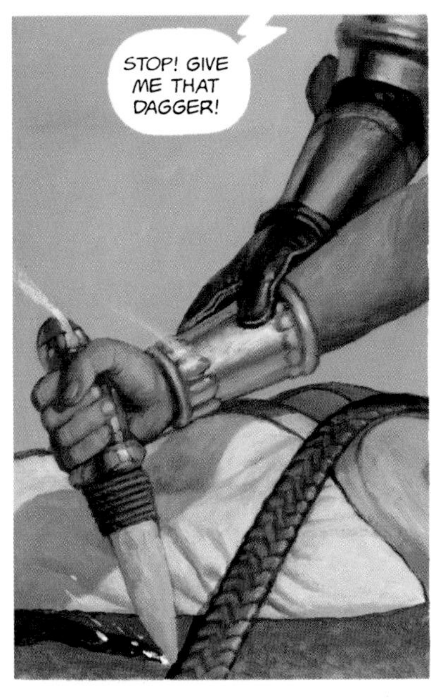
STOP! GIVE ME THAT DAGGER!

AS ENVOY OF KUKULKAN, I RECLAIM THE RIGHT TO PERFORM THE SACRIFICE.

SO BE IT.

GIVE ME THE VESSEL!

BY ALL THE GODS! THE GIRL'S NOT BREATHING!

KY, IT'S THE MERCENARY. WE'RE SURROUNDED BY GUARDS, AND I HAVEN'T GOT ANY PLAN TO GET OUT OF HERE. CAN YOU HEAR ME?
YES, I ALREADY RECOGNIZED YOUR VOICE.

I'LL SET YOU LOOSE. PLAY DEAD. DO YOU KNOW A WAY OUT OF HERE?
YES, THE DOOR BEHIND THE KING. DON'T FORGET MY WEAPON.

WHAT IS THE MEANING OF THIS? YOU DARE TO OFFEND KUKULKAN BY OFFERING A DEAD HEART?

IT CAN'T BE! HIGH PRIEST, TEST HER.

NO. ONLY THE KING MAY CONTRADICT AN ENVOY OF KUKULKAN. I WILL CARRY THE GIRL UP MYSELF. BUT YOUR DOUBT WILL COST YOU DEARLY.

KY, UP THERE YOU'LL SEE AN OBSIDIAN DAGGER. AS SOON AS YOU'RE NEAR THE KING, DO WHAT YOU LIKE WITH IT, BUT MAKE SURE YOU HAVE HIM PRIMED!

THE GIRL IS ALIVE. WHAT DO YOU MEAN?!
I TELL YOU SHE'S DEAD. LOOK CLOSER.

YOU ARE A STINKING FRIEND OF THE ATLANTEANS!

AGGG!

WHAT JUST STUCK YOU IN THE CROTCH IS A VERY SHARP KNIFE. MAKE ONE WRONG MOVE OR CRY OUT, AND IT'LL BE THE LAST THING YOU EVER DO.
YEAH, YOU HEARD RIGHT. NOW, VERY SLOWLY, TURN TOWARD THE DOOR BEHIND YOU.

WHAT IS THE MEANING OF THIS?!
DAMN IT TO HELL!

THE KING JUST GAVE THE ALARM. WARRIORS WILL BE HERE SOON, BUT WITH THAT GIZMO OF YOURS, WE CAN EASILY HANDLE THEM.
THIS "GIZMO" DOESN'T WORK ANYMORE. I JUST USED UP THE LAST ENERGY CHARGE. COME ON, FOLLOW ME. EVERYTHING'S JUST THE WAY THE BLIND MAN DESCRIBED IT.

A BLIND MAN WITH A LANTERN ON THE END OF A STICK?
THAT'S RIGHT. HE BROUGHT ME FOOD, AND HE HAD A PLAN TO SAVE ME, BUT SOMETHING WENT WRONG.

THAT SEAL LOCKS IT FROM THE INSIDE. LET'S GO, QUICKLY!

OBVIOUSLY THEY SEAL PEOPLE UP IN HERE ALIVE.

CRAM

"A SLAB OF STONE BEHIND THE SARCOPH-AGUS, UNDERNEATH THE FOOT WITH THE ANKLE BRACELET."

THAT'S IT. LIFT IT UP.

WE'VE GOT TO MAKE SURE NOT TO LEAVE ANY TRACKS.
WE NEED A LAMP.

IT GOES DOWN REALLY DEEP. AT THE END THERE'S A STAIRWAY.

THESE GODDAMN FEATHERS...

CLAK!

IN HERE, MERCENARY.

AT THIS RATE, WE SHOULD BE DOWN TO HELL SOON.
BY THE LOOK OF THINGS, THERE ARE A BUNCH OF DIFFERENT CRYPTS THAT NONE OF THE PEOPLE AROUND HERE KNOW ABOUT.

THE BLIND MAN DIDN'T TELL ME THERE WERE TWO DOORS.
LOOK, I SEE LIGHT DOWN AT THE END.

MY GOD!

THAT CAN'T BE THE WAY OUT...IT LOOKS MORE LIKE AN ENTRANCE.

WHAT IF IT'S THE ENTRANCE TO THE REAL CITY OF THE ATLANTEANS?
IT WOULD MAKE SENSE ... CAREFUL, SOMEONE'S COMING.

IT LOOKS LIKE HE'S INVITING US IN.

THAT'S NOT REAL. IT'S AN ARTIFICIAL IMAGE. BESIDES, THAT GUY IS NOT AN ATLANTEAN, I CAN ASSURE YOU.

THEN WHO IS HE?
I HAVE NO IDEA. HE MUST BE FROM ANOTHER SOLAR SYSTEM.

I SAY LET'S GO IN. THIS IS UNBE-LIEVABLE!
IT LOOKS LIKE A DAMNED TRICK TO ME...

CAREFUL. THIS ISN'T THE WAY. COME THROUGH HERE QUIETLY.
WHAT THE?!
HUH?!

VOICES WILL ACTIVATE DANGEROUS MECHANISMS. IT'S THE GATE OF A SHIP FROM ANOTHER PLANET, WHICH ARRIVED THOUSANDS OF YEARS AGO AND WAS PERHAPS THE SOURCE OF THE CONTINENT'S CULTURES. WE DISCOVERED IT YEARS AGO BUT HAVE KEPT IT SECRET.

YOU MUST FORGIVE ME, KY. I COULDN'T DO AS I'D PLANNED AND FREE YOU FROM THE TEMPLE. THERE WERE GUARDS EVERY-WHERE. FORTUNATELY, THIS WAR-RIOR STEPPED IN.
I GUESS YOU'VE FIGURED OUT THAT I'M NOT BLIND.

IN THIS CITY THEY TREAT THE BLIND VERY WELL, AND THAT'S BEEN THE ONLY WAY TO SUR-VIVE. MY HAIR AND PALE EYES WOULD HAVE GIVEN ME AWAY.

OUR OBSESSION WITH STAYING TOGETHER, ISOLATED, DAMAGED US GENETICALLY TO THE POINT WHERE WE WERE ALMOST ALBINOS.

IT'S SAFE TO GO OUT, DON'T WORRY.
OK, BUT WE'RE STILL TRAPPED IN THE MID-DLE OF THE JUNGLE. WE NEED TO GET MY FLYING ANIMAL BACK SO WE CAN ESCAPE. I HOPE THERE'S SOME WAY TO DO THAT, BECAUSE I HAVE A RENDEZ-VOUS TO KEEP IN THE MIDDLE OF THE OCEAN.

NO WAY I CAN SEE...
WELL, HOW DID YOU GET HERE?
IN A SMALL, THROWN-TOGETHER EMERGENCY BOAT, WHICH FELL APART SHORTLY AFTER WE LANDED. BUT BEFORE THAT I WAS IN WHAT'S LEFT OF ATLANTIS.

ATLANTIS....IF YOU'RE HEADED THERE AND YOU ACCEPT ME AS A TRAVELING COMPANION, I CAN OFFER YOU A FLYING SHIP TO CROSS THE OCEAN IN.
YOU'RE ON.

WE WILL GO TO MY CITY. IT'S TO THE EAST, ON TOP OF THAT MOUNTAIN. THIS PATH GOES THERE.

MY ANCESTORS GOT ALONG WELL WITH THE NATIVES FOR CENTURIES; EVEN THE ARISTOCRACY ADOPTED OUR LANGUAGE. THE MAYANS WERE CULTURED AND PEACEFUL, BUT THEN CAME THE TOLTECS, SAVAGE AND AGGRESSIVE WARRIORS FROM THE NORTH, WHO TOOK OUR PEOPLE PRISONER AND SACRIFICED THEM. THE SITUATION COULDN'T GO ON. WE DECIDED TO FLEE, AND WE BUILT A FLYING BOAT. A FEW YEARS AGO, WHEN WE WERE ALL READY TO LEAVE, THE CURRENT KING ASCENDED TO THE THRONE, AND HIS FIRST ORDER WAS TO EXTERMINATE US.

I'M THE ONLY ONE LEFT.

I WAS THINKING- THE FIRST PLACE THEY'LL LOOK FOR US IS IN YOUR CITY.
YES, BUT I DON'T SEE ANYONE FOLLOWING US, AND THIS IS THE MOST DIRECT PATH BETWEEN THE TWO CITIES.

THERE IT IS. WE HAVE TO GO TOWARD THAT WATERFALL.

WE CALL THIS THE RESERVOIR OF HOPE.

HERE IT IS.

THERE'S A SECRET DOOR THAT'S VERY TIGHT. I'LL NEED YOUR KNIFE TO OPEN IT.

THE SOLDIERS HAVEN'T FOUND IT. THE AIRSHIP IS UNDISTURBED.

AGH!!

THE SHIP, KY...EVERYTHING'S READY...THE LEVERS, IN ORDER...FROM THE LEFT...TWENTY SECONDS AFTER THE LAST ONE... DON'T TOUCH...ANYTHI--

HA! WHAT A GREAT DAY! I FINISH OFF THE LAST ATLANTEAN AND FIND THE ENTRANCE TO HIS SECRET TEMPLE.
AS FOR YOU TWO, I HAVE OTHER PLANS. YOU'LL PAY FOR HUMILIATING ME AT THE TEMPLE.

HE'S DEAD, KY. GET BEHIND ME AND STAY THERE.

NOW WE NEED THAT DRAGON MORE THAN EVER. WE WON'T GET OUT OF THIS SITUATION UNLESS WE CAN GET THAT BASTARD TO DISMOUNT.

YOU FILTHY RAT, GET OFF MY MOUNT RIGHT NOW, IF YOU DON'T WANT TO FEEL THE POWER OF KUKULKAN.
YOUR POWER?! YOU PHONY, LET'S SEE IF YOU CAN STOP THIS!

CLANG!

JUST BECAUSE YOUR ARMADILLO SUIT STOPS ARROWS, THAT'S NOT POWER. MY ARMY WILL BE HERE AT ANY MOMENT, AND THEY'LL PULL YOU OUT OF IT LIKE A A SNAIL FROM ITS SHELL.
YOU HEARD HIM, MERCENARY. IF YOU'RE GOING TO MAKE A MOVE, NOW'S THE TIME.
I'LL HAVE TO TAKE A CHANCE.

GRRR...

WHOA!

HUH? WHAT'S HAPPENING TO HIM? BY ALL THE DEMONS OF HELL! FLY HIGHER, HIGHER!

IAYK!
CRAK!

DAMN IT, WHAT DID YOU FEED HIM? HE'S NEVER FAILED TO SEE AN OBSTACLE.
JUST SOME COCA LEAVES. HE WOULDN'T OBEY ME.

THERE ARE A LOT OF REASONS TO KILL YOU, BUT THAT'S ENOUGH RIGHT THERE.
NOT SO FAST, MERCENARY. LOOK.

MY ELITE ARCHERS. THEIR ARROWS WILL PIERCE YOUR SUIT.

TELL THEM TO GET OUT OF HERE AND YOU JUST MIGHT MAKE IT OUT OF THIS WITH YOUR LIFE, WORM!
TOO LATE. THEY HAVE ORDERS TO SHOOT.

WHAT THE?!

AAAH!!
ZIP!
ZIP!

WHAT ARE YOU DOING?! GET BEHIND ME! THIS IS GETTING SERIOUS!
THEY'RE NOT AFTER US. IF THEY HAD WANTED TO, THEY WOULD HAVE PUT AN ARROW INTO EACH OF YOUR EYES. THIS IS JUST A GOOD 'OLE COUP!

WE HAVE NOTHING AGAINST YOU. GIVE US THE KING'S BODY AND WE'LL GO.

BUT IF YOU'RE STILL HERE TOMORROW, YOU WILL BE SACRIFICED.

THEY'RE GONE. BUT IT'S VERY CLEAR. THEY'LL BLAME THE KING'S DEATH ON US, SO WE'VE GOT TO DISAPPEAR. WHAT'S MORE, THEY'VE ROBBED ME OF EVERYTHING. WE'VE GOT TO FIND THIS SUPPOSEDLY FLYING CONTRAPTION.

COME ON, MERCENARY. IF IT'S SOMETHING THAT CAN FLY, THEN I CAN FIGURE OUT HOW TO FLY IT.

THIS CAN'T BE THE SHIP.
NO.

MAYBE THEY'RE SUPPLIES. THEY MIGHT COME IN HANDY.

THEY'RE ASHES.

YES, THE ATLANTEANS HAD THE CUSTOM OF SAVING THE ASHES OF THEIR DEAD. I WOULDN'T BE SURPRISED IF ALL OF THEM ARE RESTING IN THIS TEMPLE.
A CEMETERY... LET'S MAKE OUR VISIT BRIEF!

WE'VE BEEN LOOKING FOR A WHILE NOW, AND SO FAR NOTHING. I'M STARTING TO WORRY.
WELL, IT'S ALL STARTING TO MAKE SENSE TO ME.

REALLY?...WAIT, I KNOW THIS STUFF.

*A PULSE REACTOR IS A SIMPLE REACTION ENGINE WITHOUT TURBINES, WHICH NEEDS PREVIOUS VELOCITY IN ORDER TO WORK.

MERCENARY, YOU TAKE THE ENGINE CONTROLS AND I'LL TAKE THE STEERING. STRAP YOURSELF IN TIGHT.

SOUNDS LIKE IT'S PARTY TIME IN THE CITY...

TAM TAM TAM TAM

FOURTEEN...FIF-TEEN...MY GOD! WE'RE LOSING PARTS!
IT HAS TO BE INTEN-TIONAL. THE PARTS BREAKING AWAY LET US ENTER THE OPEN AIR.

...AND TWENTY. LEVER TWO!

RRRRRT...T...T
HEAR THAT? THE ENGINES ARE WORKING!

NINETEEN... AND TWENTY. LEVER THREE ACTIVATED.

WE'VE LEVELED OFF, BUT SOMETHING'S NOT RIGHT. WE DON'T HAVE ENOUGH VELOCITY. WE'RE OK FOR THE MOMENT, WITH INERTIA AND ALL, BUT IF GOD DOESN'T HELP US OUT SOON, WE'RE GOING TO CRASH INTO THOSE TEMPLES OR FALL INTO THE JUNGLE THE MOMENT WE TRY TO MANEUVER.

BUT THE MOTORS ARE WORKING!
I THINK THE THIRD LEVER DIDN'T WORK! WE DON'T HAVE ENOUGH THRUST.

THRUST! NOW I GOT IT! THE POWER IS NOT A WEAPON! THIS IS A DAMN ROCKET CHI-NESE STYLE! AND I DISCON-NECTED THE FUSE!

KY, KEEP US ALOFT. IT'S A MATTER OF SECONDS.
I CAN'T DO ANYTHING. IT'S FLYING ITSELF.

TAM TAM TA

MAYAN PEOPLE! THE FALSE ENVOY OF KUKULKAN HAS KILLED OUR KING! THE STARS SAY THAT THE PRINCE MUST NOW BE OUR KING!

HIGH PRIEST! WHY ARE THE PEOPLE FLEEING? WHAT'S THAT NOISE?

LOOK! LOOK, YOUR EXCEL-LENCY!

BOW DOWN, SIRE. THIS CAN ONLY BE DEATH!
NO, IT'S THE ANGER OF THE ATLANTEAN GODS. THEY'RE COMING BACK FOR REVENGE.

'AND SURE ENOUGH, THE SILVER-PLATED GODS RETURNED IN THE FORM OF MEN WITH FOUR FEET, FLOATING HOUSES, STICKS THAT SPAT FIRE, AND COUNTLESS OTHER MARVELS: THE CONQUISTADORES.

MERCENARY, WE'VE BEEN UP HERE A LONG TIME. ARE YOU SURE WE'LL FIND THE ISLAND FLYING BY DEAD RECKONING?
OF COURSE. BUT YOU SEE THAT HUGE WAVE? IT GIVES ME THE FEELING THAT THE PROPHECIES HAVE COME TRUE AND THAT ATLANTIS IS DISAP-PEARING UNDER THE SEA.

LOOK AT THE HORIZON. THAT CON-FIRMS MY SUSPICIONS.

YOU THINK NAN-TAY IS HERE?
SHE'S SUPPOSED TO BE HERE WITHIN A COUPLE OF DAYS, BUT YOU NEVER KNOW. LET'S TAKE A LOOK AROUND.

DON'T GO ANY NEARER. IT COULD BE DANGEROUS.

I DON'T KNOW WHAT'S HAPPENING. THE CONTROLS AREN'T RESPONDING.

WE'RE GETTING SUCKED IN, AND WE'RE FALLING INTO THE LOW PRESSURE AREA. THE LACK OF OXYGEN HAS MADE THE ENGINES CUT OUT. OH MY GOD! STRAP YOURSELF IN!
ONLY THE ROCKET COULD PULL US OUT OF THIS IN A HURRY. BUT WE'D NEED TEN MEN TO CHARGE IT UP!

WHAT WAS THAT BANG?
I DON'T KNOW...A FRAGMENT MAY HAVE JUST HIT US.

IT KNOCKED US HIGHER-- WE'RE RISING IN CIRCLES. CENTRIFUGAL FORCE IS MAKING US SPIN OUT-WARD, AND IT'LL THROW US OUT OF THIS INFERNO IF WE DON'T MELT FIRST!

WE'RE OUT, FINALLY!

WE'VE GOT TO GET AWAY FROM HERE SOMEHOW, OR ELSE WE'LL GET SUCKED IN AGAIN. MAYBE WITH A LITTLE EXTRA NUDGE...

LOOK! THE PORT WING! IT'S ON FIRE!

NOW I GET IT. THE WINGS HAVE HYDROGEN TANKS IN THEM. WHEN THEY LOSE PRESSURE, THE FLAMES WILL GET INSIDE AND THE WING WILL EXPLODE!

BOOM

WE'RE GOING TO FALL IN THE CRATER!

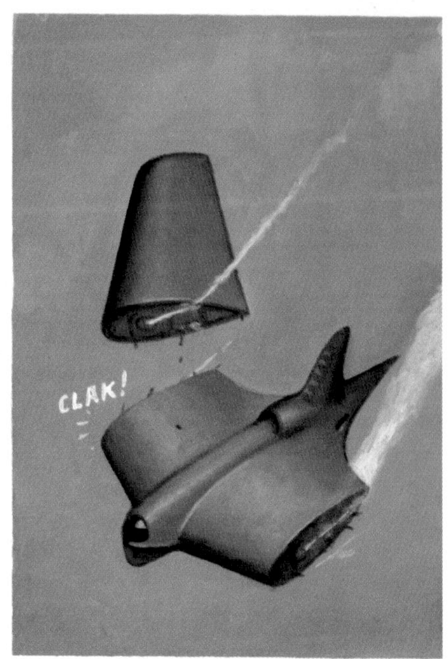
CLAK!

KY! DAMN! WE'VE LOST THE OTHER WING!
IT WAS BOUND TO HAPPEN. BUT WE'RE DROPPING FASTER.

THERE'S NO MORE DIS-PLACEMENT MASS, AND I CAN'T RAISE THE BOW OF THE SHIP. WE'RE GOING TO CRASH!

FOOMSS...

THAT'S IT...CAN'T HOLD ON...GOT TO LET HIM GO, OR I'LL DIE WITH HIM.

THE DOME...IT'S A MIRACLE.

I CAN'T FIND THE ISLAND. I'M LOST.

I COULDN'T HAVE MISSED BY SO FAR...UNLESS IT'S ALL BEEN SUB-MERGED.

WHAT'S THAT GLOW OVER THERE?

I CAN'T GO ON, MERCENARY. WE'VE SPENT DAYS KEEPING A LIGHT IN THE DOME.
THAT LIGHT WILL SAVE OUR LIVES... AND PRAY IT DOESN'T GET CLOUDY.

THE ISLAND DISAPPEARED TWO DAYS AGO. SHE WON'T SEE US.
THAT'S WHAT YOU THINK. NAN-TAY IS A VERY GOOD PILOT.

ALL RIGHT--BUT IN THESE TWO DAYS, WHO KNOWS HOW FAR WE'VE DRIFTED WITH THE CURRENT. WE'D PROBABLY HAVE BEEN BETTER OFF DROWNING.
STOP! YOU'RE CHEERING ME UP!
45

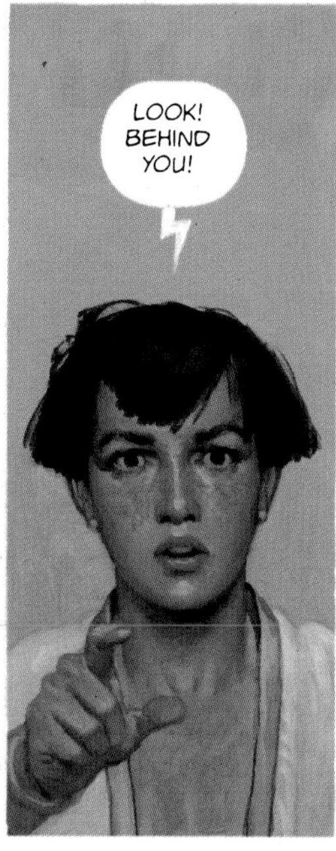
LOOK! BEHIND YOU!

THANK GOD! I HOPE SHE'S GOT WATER.
DON'T FOOL YOUR-SELF. IF SHE'S GOT WATER IT'S FOR THE MOUNT.

WHAT A SURPRISE, MERCENARY. YOU'RE MORE THAN A HUNDRED KILOMETERS FROM OUR MEETING PLACE. YOU SHOULD THANK THE LIGHT IN THE DOME.

NAN-TAY, THIS IS KY.
KY? THE KY FROM MY PLANET?

BY ALL THAT'S HOLY, I DON'T KNOW HOW YOU ENDED UP HERE, BUT I ASSURE YOU YOU'RE WELCOME.

THIS MEANS THAT OUR PLANET IS STILL IN A MATCHING ORBIT WITH THE EARTH.
YES. THE CONTROL ROOM BRAIN GAVE ME ANOTHER OPTION, AND I CAME THROUGH OK, EVEN THOUGH THE PLANET STAYED CONTAMINATED. BUT I WAS SO ALONE, AND THOSE MYTHOLOGICAL BEINGS WERE SO UNPLEASANT...

YOU WEREN'T ALONE. BESIDES THE MYTHOLOGICAL ONES, THERE WAS SOMEONE ELSE.

SOMEONE ELSE? HUMANS?
ALMOST.

NAN-TAY, DID YOU FIND THE ATLANTEANS IN THE EAST?
NO, BUT I HAVE A FEW CLUES...